LETTER FROM LOS ANGELES

LETTER *from* LOS ANGELES

Poems by

CHARLES GULLANS

JOHN DANIEL AND COMPANY · SANTA BARBARA · 1990

Many of these poems first appeared in *The Hudson Review*, *The Southern Review*, *The Greensboro Review*, *The Michigan Quarterly Review*, *Drastic Measures*, *The Chicago Review*, *The Massachusetts Review*, *San Marcos Review*, *The Gramercy Review*, *Fragments*, *The New York Times*, and *Yankee*. Thanks are owed to the editors of the journals for permission to reprint. "Satyr (Chuck's, Westwood)" first appeared in *Poetry* under the title "Satyr," ©Modern Poetry Association, 1974. Others are reprinted from *Imperfect Correspondences*, *Many Houses* (The Symposium Press, 1978, 1981), *The Bright Universe* (Abbatoir, 1983), *Under Red Skies* and *Local Winds* (Robert L. Barth, 1983, 1985). Copyright ©*Yankee*, 1966; and Charles Gullans, 1978, 1981, 1983, and 1985.

Copyright ©1990 by Charles B. Gullans
All rights reserved
Printed in the United States of America

Design and typography by Jim Cook/Santa Barbara
Joshua Odell, Poetry Editor

LIBRARY OF CONGRESS CATALOGING-IN-PUBLICATION DATA
Gullans, Charles B.
    Letter from Los Angeles / Charles Gullans.
       p. cm.
    ISBN 0-936784-79-2: $8.95
    I. Title.
PS3513.U73L4   1990
811'.54—DC20   89-27908 CIP

Published by John Daniel & Company, Publishers
Post Office Box 21922
Santa Barbara, California 93121

Distributed by Texas Monthly Press
Post Office Box 1569
Austin, Texas 78767

Letter from Los Angeles

1	Letter from Los Angeles
2	John Wilkes
4	Calvin in the Casino
6	Research
8	Labuntur Anni
10	The Other Room
12	In Proprios Greges
13	A Faust for the Seventies: A Farewell
15	Anti-Faust
17	Many Houses: 1-10
28	Burnt Offerings of 1975
30	Broken Wings
32	Poet to Poet
34	Fête Galante
36	Local Winds: 1-7
43	Gunsmoke
44	Letters Home
45	In the Marina
46	The Chart House
47	A Roof in Islamabad
48	Moscow Suburban Nights
50	Los Angeles Place Names
59	Metaphysics at Twenty-Six

60 Imperfect Correspondences
66 Adagia
67 Measures
68 Terra Cognita
70 Remembered Landscape
71 The House of Exile

Letter from Los Angeles

Poems by Charles Gullans

Letter from Los Angeles

But here the autumn falls to soft November.
The warm rain by a warm wind loosely driven
Starts the mild ecstasy of leaf and flower.
Outside my door, the thrusting bamboo loosens
Branches and branching leaves, and paper trees,
Swollen with their swift, cellular explosions,
Spread vaster in the night. Wild in confusion,
The orange and lime are blossoming and bearing.
I pick the fruit from branches in full bloom.
From rind and flesh, from stamen and corolla,
The pungencies of fruit and flower invade
My senses with their vegetable contagion
Until I almost sleep within their bright,
Alluring indistinction, almost merge
With the corrupted and corrupting season.
Then in a silence that no wind relieves,
The moisture of the parting eyelid clicks,
The breath, indrawn, is heard, if distantly.
These are the merest whispers in the mind,
But sounds that will assert their own temptation
And call me from the ambiance of the leaves;
Call to withdraw and, in returning, claim
Precise enjoyments of the appetite,
Known imperfections of the human will,
The old corruptions of the blood and brain.

John Wilkes

Lord Bute, whose rant was the establishment,
Had studied and had mastered the appearance
Of public virtue, but his private bent
Was mistresses and whores built for endurance.

The public interest hid his private acts.
His principle, self-interest of the few,
The fool aristocrat, he hated facts
And any man of strong, contrary view.

But here was Wilkes, the upstart gentleman,
Bourgeois, with an aristocrat's disdain
Of canting ethics and of rant in one,
Or in the many, whom he hoped to gain.

"I have no minor vices," though a boast,
  Was license to quick, brittle fools to laugh;
Then, teaching what hyperbole may cost,
  His wit pursued him like an epitaph.

No hypocrite, his vices all well known,
"Godless, but never womanless an hour,"
Hard and contemptuous, still the man had grown
Hating restriction and abusive power.

Consistency is firmness in each type.
Yet men of principle may simply be—
Hero or saint, coward or guttersnipe—
Persistent in the partial good they see.

Then if defect seems equal in each eye,
Prefer the cynic to the hypocrite.
Despise the Bute who said to him, "You'll die
Of syphilis or on the gallows yet."

Prefer the Wilkes who looked into that face,
And with the swift inconscience of the bored
Said, "That depends on whether I embrace
Your mistress or your principles, my Lord."

Calvin in the Casino

after a poem by Turner Cassity

Brief model of our spinning universe,
Your motions random and your judgment terse,

Definitive as grace or as damnation,
In tedious compelling permutation,

How meaningless the calculus of chance
Which tells us all, yet nothing in advance:

Abstract and actuarial, the tables
Yield us a knowledge that almost disables.

Repetitive, the numbers hold our eyes,
Autistic visions, here, of paradise.

Here in the click and tumble of the balls,
All merit is to him on whom it falls.

Inscrutably, predicted by no art,
The infinite momentum of the heart—

Racked on the motions of the faltering wheel,
The benedictions of predestined steel—

Spins to the counsels of perfection where
Experience and knowledge teach despair.

Induction leaps its fragile evidence
From Chance through Fortune, thence to Providence,

Random, benign, malign, or God's Decrees.
We stand transfixed by probabilities.

Knowledge is ignorance in fine detail:
Who know for certain that at last they fail,

Know nothing else will help them in this place,
And pray for chance to help them, pray for grace.

Research

> *Not all facts are historical facts.* —E.H. CARR

We search through lives for the exemplary,
For shapes that have some meaning; and we see,

Scrawled in obscure, obscene ephemera,
Drift without aim. Terrors of trivia,

The necessary wastes to be endured,
Like cosmic sequences of the absurd,

Push to exhausted sleep. So let it be:
"Unsought particular addressing me,

Are you the change allotted to my shape,
Or messenger of chaos, jaws agape

And speaking words I almost understand?"
No one can read the lives of the unmanned.

Turn it around: the ghost confronting you
And crying for your blood is simply you,

The shadow thrown by every future act,
The to be willed or to be unwilled act.

It is ourselves we judge, that we condemn
Or know or modify, when we face them,

The men we were not and could never be,
Though archetypes of our own history.

These are inverted horoscopes we cast,
It is ourselves we summon from the past.

Labuntur Anni

The years estrange, leaving impassive aims,
A hardened will, and loneliness;
The years divide us, as and when they will,
From youth and pride, then from our modest claims
To dignity and deference, to less
Than the least measure we had hoped to fill.

All choices narrow to some lesser scope:
Desire, the long deferred, is least recalled,
Love, the renewer, absent from our schemes.
The future we laid up in monstrous hope,
And till this time by time itself forstalled,
Arrives like terror in our nightly dreams.

The years divide, and yet the years fulfill:
The past we laid down carelessly returns
With gifts more stunning than the future seemed
When it held everything in promise still.
In the ironic grace of time, one learns
That, gift by gift, all losses are redeemed,

And blessings issue from their stony faces.
The gift of pain precedes humility,
The gift of loss unburdens of possession;
Malice, deceit, betrayal—each displaces
Ignorance, pride, and brute naivete;
And death, the welcome gift of intercession.

But if the gifts seem less a gift than rod
Of our unsought and undesired fears,
Stranger the blessings given to our keeping:
Blesséd the blind for they shall see no tears
Blesséd the deaf for they shall hear no weeping,
Blesséd the dumb for they shall not curse God.

The Other Room

The room upstairs is empty. I hear sound,
But an old building, settling, makes such sound
As is the merest whisper in the mind.
It is the kind of sound old buildings make
Beyond the edge of meanings that we know,
Troubling the ear with hints, with shades, and signs
That stay what they have been, sounds that reply
Nothing to our persistent questioning.

There are whole schools of vague interpreters,
The scholiasts of hope, who say they know
The invisible inhabitants of air,
And know the lord of those old messengers,
Sufficient to their faith. They know, at least,
Their mortal terror of the old abyss
Who spin from frail analogies of sense—
Their other rooms—proofs of what eye and ear
Cannot perceive. But let them be. Let be.

Their inclination to disturb the dark,
The shuttered room above, cannot disturb
Our tenancy here on the floor below.
The house may creak and shudder to the storms
That rage down from the upper atmosphere,
And horror seem to settle. Do not fear.
The room upstairs is empty. Though I hear
The rumors of the old inhabitants,
I hear the simple sound and nothing more.
The other room is locked to inquiry.
We dwell here in God's darkness. Let it be.

In Proprios Greges

That you exist is all I need to know.
It does not matter on what road I go,

You are forever elsewhere, far ahead
Or passing backward to a place I fled.

I, who desire your knowledge, know your face
As a vanished presence in an empty space.

Whom should I speak to, ask, indemnify
For answer to this agony, or lie

Which cannot be refuted nor be proved?
All answers seem with time but more removed.

Although you do not answer when I call,
Words less than yours are as no words at all.

You do not, or you will not, speak to me,
But let your mystery and your silence be,

The hooded wanderers of the zodiac,
Who leave but airy footsteps in their track.

A Faust for the Seventies:
A Farewell

Fifty and fey, he reads another book,
And then another he has read before,
And ponders nothing from his inglenook
So deep as the glass that he will fill once more.

The aging scholar, deep in his duress
And dryness, reads another dried up page;
The aging lover, bound to less and less,
Picks up a cigarette and lights it, sage

In nothing quite so much as his own case
And pity for the sadness of his time,
Which made him what he is, a bitter face,
In whom the tooth of anger works like lime.

He thinks too little and he thinks too much,
Too little of the work that he should do;
But times are troubled and the times are such,
He's always thinking of his losses, too.

With resolution heightened by the wine,
He finds a use for learning and for fears.
Some dim election working in his mind
Whispers the words to ransom his lost years.

He draws the signs of power with chalky squeaks,
Draws his own blood and watches as it dries,
Then makes the ancient sacrifice, and speaks
The words of power unto the Lord of Flies.

A devil, small and personal, appears
Within the pentagram, his horns and tail
Both faintly barbed with malice and arrears,
Who lights a cigarette from his own nail,

Exhales, and watches as the thin smoke weaves,
And strikes his hooves upon the floor to bow.
"I bring you greetings from the Prince of Thieves,
Your life is not worth changing. End it now."

Anti-Faust

You by the fireplace, your glass of whiskey
Set on my mantelpiece, a little frisky

As you are speaking of your long success
And probing in my depths of idleness,

Smooth talker, you, you Shakespeare of men's hearts,
Now turned Catullus of the nether parts,

I hear the offer you are making me,
As crude and brutal as pure sex would be

Without the love that should attend it. You,
First Author of Conversion, know how true

And vulgar images engage weak sense,
Consuming us with promise of the intense

And promises of power. But that's a lure
I can resist. Why not try something sure

And obvious that no one could refuse,
An endless wallet, say? And I could use

Something much rarer, Father of Alcohol,
A bar companion I could stand at all,

A waiter who refuses tips, a cop
Who calls me sir, an honest body shop.

I should not ask, instead I should be thanking
You for what you have given, Father of Banking,

Father of All Insurance, Uncle Tom's
And Aunt Jemima's, Father of Uniforms,

And Dum-Dum Bullets, and Close Order Drill,
And Gatling Guns, you Eater of All Swill.

The gifts I need, I may find yet in time,
And I may not. Yours have their birth in slime,

Father of Napalm. Turn away your face,
Finish your drink, and leave my fireplace.

Many Houses

Part I

1.

I'm home and finding the Los Angeles
Nobody loves where everybody lives,
The concrete miles that crouch beneath Bel Air
And Brentwood to the sea, if living is the word
For bare accommodation in these rooms
With nothing that we do not bring to them.
In the impersonal we make some life
With a few sticks and rags, a bed, a chair,
Some pottery, some pictures, and the phone.
No attics and no basement, thus, no past;
No history, therefore no legacy.
Transience is not symbolic, it is real
In the unfurnished places of our lives
So bare of ghosts, so barren of plain hope
A man would welcome the implacable
To live here, too, goddesses underground,
The Furies who pursue, but also bless,
Who are the mind and meaning of the past.
Here there is nothing deeper than the dust
That settled yesterday. Think of the mind
That shaped these rooms, and think what they will shape—
These narrow, mean, anonymous white walls,
These low-built roofs—in human penury,
In dearth and destitution. Ugliness
Bestrides whole lives and twists them to its ends.

2.

These rooms were built for the large gesture, friends
In multitude, dinner and candlelight,
And old books open on the study floor.
The wine uncorked and glasses filled, I wonder
Will we make love here? Will the imaged walls
Contain us in the privacy of peace
And benediction? The archaic smile
Might beckon us to its secure delights
With radiance and candor, to repose
In love and its embodiments, to sleep
In warmth and trust. Gods and generic Greeks
Are drifting round the room, woman and girl,
Man and boy, splendidly, lush and compact.
There in the clearness of the photograph,
Sea-risen, she, and mother of us all,
The sperm-born rides, as my hand rounds your back,
And curves your thigh, my lips upon your lips.
I am seducing you and you seduce
With amiable indifference to the nude
Divinities and chorus-line of youth
Across the wall. My home-made gallery,
My shrine to old religion, bothers you
Not in the least. Gods smile on me and you,
The once bare walls, the fierce activity
Upon the floor. Love and its ironies
Occur where they occur and can be taken,
And lovers take the blessings they are given.

3.
I waken to your breathing in the night
And feel you stir beneath my hand, alive,
Responsive to the questioning. You turn
And make your turning last forever. Then,
Slowly, as we invade each other's senses,
I enter you. You enter me. We two
Dissolve into each other's surfaces.
We linger. We withdraw. We merge a while
And reemerge to what is just occurring.
I know what I desire of you, your hair,
Your hair has overwhelmed me with desire.
And then—you take me always by surprise
In blind commingling and the fiercest joy
In strength you give me and I give to you.

4.
Drinking the honored names, Château Margaux
And Haut-Brion, our talk touches a book,
A print, and they pass round the table, too,
Masters of the hard line, and strong lines, too.
An evening is set free from grim event,
From the invidious, the brutal minds
Of academic terrorists who stain
The autumn days with calumny. Dear God,
With what relief we taste the wines and hear
The gentle voices of our honored friends
Over the modulations of the music,
Filling the other room with its grave sound,
Moving and memorable. The old wines speak
In words so witty and in words so wise

They are the genius of good fellowship.
May we all come to such a growth as this
Nor falter in the dumb unreadiness
Of youth. My friends, you know my joy in you
Has not been spoken, nor my pride in you,
Who face the difficult, who say the just,
The true, who test the mettle that is man
Now in the meanness of adversity.
November has arrived, and the great wines
Are being broached. My friends, I drink to you,
And drink to a future, if not long, then rich
In love and wine, in friends and vintages.

5.
I hear you typing in the other room
Where you define your future as a life
That will exclude me. All the past is ranged
Here in this room in the coincidence
Of personal and the historical,
My memory and row on row of books,
My life and my profession. History
Is fixed in the veridical event,
And books are its brief lives, its summaries.
They are the images that shape our minds
Like standard verities, like truth itself.
I know the old persuasion in each voice
As I talk nightly with the printed pages
Telling me once again and yet once more
The same old things. The voices never change.
Event is dead. It is unalterable.
The words have never changed since they were written.

The voices now are just as soft or shrill
As they have ever been; if they are sad,
It is because I think that they are sad,
Because they tell me they are so. Your voice
Is falling word by word upon a page
In the next room, making a new event
Inalterably dead. The intimate
And personal are also true. And love,
Love which was once the fluid and unfixed,
Becomes a memoir or scenario,
Another book upon another shelf;
Another piece of minor history,
This poem on this page. In a few days
You will get up and walk across the room
And turn the handle of the door and leave,
And leave behind unalterable loss.

PART II

6. AT HOME
For all my years, for all it is a house
That I have lived in, still, each night
I push my way through passages, past walls,
Stumbling toward sleep. The unfamiliar floors
Twist like a maze, the doorposts shift
And angle in the dark. Drunk or confused,
Belligerent, I sink to the cold tiles.
What am I doing here? Where is my room,
The nightlamp and my pillow? Who is he
The blunderer inside my head whose cough
Keeps me awake, whose dreams obsess my day,
This fool without a compass in the night,
Lost in his own house, looking for his bed?

7. LIVING ALONE
Summoned from depths and distances apart,
I wake, and without thinking, dress. I go
To write my letters, read my texts, and teach,
Having, at least, to do this. Was there once,
Before the unnamed havoc spread by time,
Someone or something else, a form that answered
As friend, as lover, an activity
To which I turned in joy, giving my strength
And loyalty, facing the adverse world
With laughter and contempt.
                            The beach was warm,
The sea so cold the water bit like acid.
For days clouds over the peninsula

Held rain in high suspension, while we played
Between the running tides, and walked the shore,
Islands of shared sufficiency. At night
The warm fire moved us into dreamless sleep
And light returned us purposes as clear
And unforeboding as the seaward sky.
The steady welling of the sea became
The measure of our days.
      At night I read
What others did with their predicament,
Looking for wisdom in the gritty soil
Of one man's self, another's solitude,
And put their books aside. For all they say
Something acute or memorable or true,
Each speaks of his insoluble disease,
His own extremity.
      Here in my chair
I listen to the music fill the room
With sentiment, a joy so strenuous
It's close to tears, and wonder where it is—
In a quartet, a poem, someone's play,
A definition of what never was
Except in hope, some blessed shape we give
To clay or wood or words? The bafflement
Of purposes diffused like morning fog
Across the landscape of the years returns
As stinging as frustration. Dull and dense,
And ignorant as a child, I start all over
With a blank page before me and a pen.

8. MANY HOUSES

Too many houses and too many lives
Mixed into them. What trash and trivia!
Detritus of our daily living, heaped
High as the sills, massively undisturbed
And undisturbable, waits for us there
In its enormity all night and day.
We live forever in the midden heap
Of old emotions, where our history
Has its own tedium and tawdriness,
Defying order like a poltergeist,
The emanation of a child, disturbed
And uncontrollable in sullen fury.
What do we leave to any who inquires
But the debris of something that was ours
And irreplaceable? A broken cup
Or the egregious sorrow of lost love,
Nothing that can be mended or unmarred.

9. AFTER THE WAR

Whose voice is in the next room? Radio
Defeats the silence and assaults the frames
Of pictures on the wall, and skews the drapes
And silts the floor with dust. Whole histories
Have trampled here in script and commentary—
Ten minutes or ten words abbreviate
A decade's war to bare narration. Thus,
"Goodbye" becomes the summary of love.
And love and history speak in one voice.
"The absoluteness of accomplished fact"
Compels us all, a standard verity

To which we nod. Well, since we wage no war,
Let us wage peace, and fill this gentler time
With recapitulations of a past
Called history, or life, or yesterday;
Where, intermixed, inseparably allied,
The intimate, the personal, the true
Jostle with crude event in the large world,
Events no way reducible to mind.
Love and the past are not activity,
But subjects now for study, fixed
By words once spoken in another room,
And fluid to the mind as once to sense.
Open the windows wide to the salt breeze
And listen to the ponderous Pacific
Speak in its own slow voice, rushing the waste
Down the hard rock and sand. Its one concern
Is with today, which lacks the eloquence
Of brevity, the terseness of the past.
It is unedited and unrevised
By memory or pride or vanity.
It is the simple given that we live.
If, now, silence oppresses, still my house,
Warm in the early dusk of late October,
Is one where love has been and left behind
Its own intensities. If brief, if late,
It scarcely matters now, since I survive.
Perhaps they were a triad of the time,
When violence, unmitigated loss,
And horror day by day—insanity,
Even in the Capitol—did not surprise,
And shock lived in the air. Late, brief, intense:

If we are chastened, we are friends; we know
The gift was given in a passing time
And that it was a gift, late, brief, intense,
When many have had nothing all their lives,
And many lives no time in which to love.

10. OPEN HOUSE

The doors are open to the autumn night
And in my house, my friends are gathering,
Coming out of the night to drink the wine
That's airing in the other room, to praise
The fresh white paint and pictures on the walls
And a new vase from an old potter's hand.
The house is singing and the pictures talk
And friends are coming here to listen, speak,
And add their voices like a legacy
In laughter as robust as the red wine.
If you were in my place you'd understand
Why voices ring in every room, why sound
So permeates the rafters and the floors
I cannot walk but voices flood my ears
And flood my senses with the memories.
It is the music of my history
Echoing through the house and through my mind,
Voices from all the rooms where I have lived
And voices from the inwardness of things.
I think I've never seen a blue so deep
As in this vase, a line so elegant
As in this print; here in staggering dark
They are as luminous as love or friends,
As warming as the hand is to the wine,

As noble as our losses. What we tried
Was worth the risk of losing in the end,
And knowledge of all losses is the same.
We should be generous as is the wine,
As ample with our praise, as soft to friends,
As smooth, as supple, as harmonious.
We have survived the ignorance of our youth,
The smuttiness of our maturity,
And the thin places in the mind. As friends
We face the uncertain future while we drink.
There is such beauty in these walls as we
Shall never see again, so praise the time
That brought us to this house, these friends, these wines,
And the arrogance that kept us here alive,
Whose lives were touched briefly by the august
And terrible, by love and hate and war.

Burnt Offerings of 1975

As nervous as antennae in the night,
You hold a cigarette for me to light.

Despite the hour, despite our solitude,
Our colloquy is gentle, never crude,

Though I am stalking you. You know that's true,
As we discuss your prosody, as you

Defend experiment in verse. And find
The subject dangerous and change your mind.

There's every reason in the world that I
Given my age, my shrewd, accurate eye,

Should find you the epitome of charm,
Still there's no reason you should come to harm,

As little reason you should ever guess
I'll never move around the table. Yes,

I want to say it, so I will. I do:
Dear child of days, I am in love with you.

It was not hard to say. There it all ends
With you, you, you, your silly face and hands

I can't stop watching and can't memorize.
It does no harm to you, this rape by eyes.

It does no harm to me, to love the good
And beautiful. To love you as I should.

Broken Wings

Dinner by candlelight has always meant
Just what we know it means, so your low voice
Tells me in moving terms the slender story,
Your shyness and his tenderness in love,
Your parting. Then, late mercy for old pain,
This sympathy, this interest, this time.
A little wine and more than a few years
Have brought us here. We have become ourselves.
And have no need of cautionary tales
Told to the young. My youth is far away,
Perchance it sleepeth in some distant land
Or meditateth on some new pursuit.
I don't believe you care, and that is why
I've asked you here and why you charm me here,
And why I hope that you will come again

For other dinners and the candlelight,
For wines made memorable by sharing them.
Dear Child of years, whatever they might be,
I want you as you are, not a day less
In wit or in experience. Your face
Abides all questioning, so let us say
It is our liberty that we explore,
The gain of great good nature. You and I,
Smiling, embracing, circle once or twice,
Half-in, half-out of time with the Ballade
Before we move off down the hall to sleep,
Which, in an hour, will come as welcomely
As your compliance and your confidence,
Your silence now my hands are joined to yours,
Your haste to take me through the door to joy.

Poet to Poet

Low overhead, jet fighters range the sky,
The pilots young and accurate, the planes
As arrogant as health or summer tan,
And steady as their breathing. Autumn sun
And hazy autumn clouds divide the sky
They rule now in their great machines. I turn
From latitudes where youth and competence
Perform the works of power. I turn aside
To the bare chapel in the desert heat,
To the old friends so dumbly gathered now,
And walk inside to speak with you once more.
Do they tell you I am dying?
                    No,
They tell me you are dead, they say that chance,
Pain, fortitude, and risk have brought you here
To the unwished-for room, to this constraint,
The promised end of everything we know.
I cannot look at you. Dumb images
Are eloquent with terror, when the night
Encompasses them wholly, when the end
Is swift and violent. *Our minds are wild*
With the specific grimness of the prose,
With alien chill at words we never thought
Would be the words that we would hear of you.
Strangers? Yes, for a little while.

                              As long
As I have left to live, we are estranged
And speechless, who in life exchanged all words,
The many and the few, angry and mild.
But yet she walks beside you.
                                    Yes, in thought,
In harried memory, she still pursues
Her tenuous existence for a while.
Remember? I do.
                    Yes, and I do, too,
And that is all I do, possessing nothing,
No knowledge and no certainty of grace,
No words of power to stay you here or ease
Your passage to occlusion and eclipse.
You belong to dusk,
                      and so to me
As no one else; as fathers to their daughters,
So mothers to their sons. Dear loss, dear earth,
I will not come to visit you again.
Someone will always hear it.
                              Say farewell.

Fête Galante

The gifts are fewer, but they're more intense
At fifty. Think of the absurd, immense

Collation that awaits us at *La Grange*,
Where, for a long, convivial mélange,

You—Eleanor, Victoria, and Tim—
Are taking me to dinner. Such a whim,

God knows, and such extravagant expense!
I like the lavishness of lavish friends:

The prudent leave no mark upon their time,
Nor do the liberal. You entertain

Magnificence: here's shrimp and duck, white wine,
And salad and pâté. And so we dine.

All starch and brisk command, waiters, at call,
Bring on the courses as the bottles fall,

One by one, exhausted, pale, and mute.
In each brave death, our pleasure is acute,

As is the irony of circumstance:
Such noble breed and towering elegance

To point the casual banter of our wit,
Here, double steel, and there, a charming hit.

It is a little world that you have made,
Where, for a while, the waiting shadows fade,

And stand back from the feast. I know the gift
Of moments marked out from the invidious drift

To silence. Something luminous is here.
It's more than love, because it will endure,

And more than liking, it is so intense.
It is the gift your being here presents,

Your time and your concern, which binds me fast
In the intensest spell the night can cast.

Local Winds

I. COLLOQUY BY THE FIREPLACE

Your face is so intent upon your work
This evening that I sit here quietly,
While you make notes for dialogue and sip
Your coffee. Think, as a blank piece of paper
Longs for black ink and words, so there are men
Whose constant predicate of thought is "You,"
A high abstraction answering in sense
To vivid and precise particulars
Of face and body, gesture and repose.
They speak so that another will reply,
So words will specify the cold, white wastes,
And touch may vivify their unused senses.
I was a dweller in an empty house
In a deserted countryside, and saw
Nothing at all upon the frozen plains
Beyond the lucid glass that sealed me in,
Until you gave me language, gave me words.
You named me and I answered. You returned
Old modes of feeling, dormant till your touch
Had roused me from the stoic spell of snow
And filled me up to overflowing. Love,
You never did me harm. You never could,
But I return you treason as I sit,
Watching you turn the pages of a book
You read for pleasure after hours of work
And smoke your cigarette. I think of love

And our enacting it last night. I think
Of all the generous details of love,
And know that I am false of heart, that I
Translate your fullness to a form of words,
Betraying you with my own memories,
My need to know the past, to consummate
The conquest of your body in my mind,
As though I turned our love into a book,
A story in some sweet, unlikely past.

2. THE FIRST HERESY

I know, I know the rhetoric of extremes,
The rituals of desire. Joy in your arms
Is joy in plenitude, and love fulfilled,
Yet still I hesitate. This afternoon
I was too moved to speak to you at all,
But watched you, gravely smiling, while you talked
To guests I wished would vanish, and you moved
Through sunlight and through shadow by the pool,
As slowly as you walk, now, with my hand
In your hand to our room. The afternoon
Has served us very well with its delay,
Deepening the shadows and the silent rooms.
Of ordinary noise, of people living,
Drinking and gossiping, filling the house
With bustle and to-do—of other lives,
We've had enough today. In a slow voice,
I speak to you of many ways of love,
And in a little while, we shall lie down,
And we will learn of all of them. Tonight,
Tomorrow, and tomorrow, we are flesh,

We are incarnate names; and we speak tongues
Of revelation, flame upon our lips.
And we are in one place with one accord.
Turn to me now, and I will worship here.
I am so filled to utterance that I
Propound divinity from sacred texts
Of brow and lip. The gift of tongues descends
And I declare its meaning in this kiss.

   3. GOING TO BED
"The metaphysics of the id are crude,"
You tell me, as I wash my face and hands;
And taking down a towel from the rack,
I ask you, "Are you reading from a book?"
And you say, "Yes, it is the character
I've made you in the first act of the play.
You are the key to the catastrophe,
You guide the talking on its friendly course
To recognition and unraveling."
I box you playfully around the room
And laughing into bed and underneath
The sheets at last. Dear friend, unravel this,
How well we fit in this asexual,
Least usable position, back to front,
My hand around and light upon your chest,
And tapping out the rhythm of a thought,
My nose deep in the fragrance of your hair,
The comfort of your skin. I understand,
You understand how very close we are
To the imperial power. Your gentle touch,
The reassurances you give to me

Measure our distance from the urgent need
To try the limits of our pleasure. Sleep.
The satisfactions of the afternoon,
The taut, warm pleasures of the evening pass
Into illusions in our memories,
And we are resting in the overflow.
Sleep and his brother seem most welcome now.

4. LOCAL WINDS

I had been reading late, until I heard
The winter night come squalling, and fine rain
Sweep in from sea, and strike the paper trees
And sound the window panes. Closing my eyes,
I slipped beneath the blankets on our bed
And dozed, until a huge gust hit the walls,
And the house shuddered like a heavy ship,
Cresting on weathery seas. I woke to find
A darkness that the storm made absolute.
You have abandoned me in deepest sleep.
I know this for my own hyperbole,
As I lie lonely by your shoulder blades,
Admiring your abstractedness, and moved
To animal intensity of need
To hear you speak my name, and kiss my hand,
And touch my fingertips. No words of power
Can raise your spirit from the place of dreams,
Nor bring you up awake to fill my need
To see you stir or breathe or move some way
To reaffirm your presence in my world,
And share the loneliness of wind and rain
Or listen for the silence after storm.

Your stillness is an icon of your death;
And images too grave for intimate
And personal surrender stream in thought
Like winter rain, wild with unlooked-for loss.
Caught in the climax of this little death,
I slip back into sleep and down to depths
Where you lie dreaming of your own concerns.

5. JACOB'S LADDER
Surely some gods have settled in this place,
Archaic and benign, and we must learn
The language of their praise. The words of power
Fell to us from the air, and on our tongues
They have compelled a blessing. Gratitude
For gifts so great should be unstinting, too.
The simple words rise up in us at dawn,
The ancient words that name and praise at once.
"Surely this is the place of god," we say,
"And we have looked upon his face," we sing.
And so we praise the alien messenger
We wrestled all night long. We do not need
To ask the name. We know the youthful god,
Springing forever from his stone repose,
Who visits us by night with candid smile
And outspread wings, poised lightly on the air,
Eros the Terrible, who blesses some,
Before he folds them in his wide embrace.

6. THE RECOGNITION

The kettle steams upon the kitchen stove
As you fix each of us a cup of tea
So we can talk. And what will come of talk
Except the pleasure of your voice and mine
As they weave dialogue? The ancient signs
Are set against each other like the sound
Of music, balancing two voices, one
Above the other, dominant, secure,
Because the other matches note for note.
It is in this concordance that I learn
Your need for what I have and what I give
Of love and knowledge in a spacious house
Among the whispering trees and quiet lawns.
And this is set against all time to be.
The future comes from its vast distance here,
Because we call it here, and we embrace
Its coming on. Now like a song of love,
A chapter in a book, a cup of tea,
Something is coming surely to an end
In the bold cadence we had long foreseen,
In the last fragrance of the warm, brief cup,
The pages that we will not turn again
Of our own friendly story. Time will call
Like a great bell that sounds the silent hours,
And you will go to purposes we built
Together and of one accord for you.
And you will hasten forward, bound and rapt
To your own music ringing in your ears,
As all the future lies there in the leaves
Upon the bottom of two empty cups.

7. FOREIGN TRAVEL

I thought I saw your broad back in the crowd,
As sharp and casual as a photograph,
Head turned to look for traffic, your whole weight
Held on one foot, there on a London curb.
So habit travels with us. Then for weeks
I saw the same back and the same poised
Expectancy of motion. If I forgot,
It came again, your apparition—lost,
I knew quite well, five thousand miles away—
There in the bearing of some innocent,
Who briefly bore my love, and walked away
Into another story and a plot
With different purposes. Swift images
Of body in its motion and repose
Will burn into our senses, set their shape
In the deep rifts of feeling, and rise up
Like demons to possess us. For a while,
I thought about the picture in my mind,
The story as it was, with all your charm
Of surfaces and fine anatomy.
And what are they? In truth they were the lure
That led me to the house of mirth and joy
And pleasure where it lives. A candid shot
Now worn to the simplicity of stone
A photograph, recessed within the mind.
But what of these appearances on streets,
Real imitations of remembered things,
Of places, people, you? I give it up,
And cling to what I know. I know the grace
Of loving you was simply this: you gave,
And gave again until the gift was bounty,
A superflux I live in every day.

Gunsmoke

The wide brim of my hat turns slightly up
To shade the sun from my face. Like a cup

It drinks up shadows, where I walk the street,
Impersonal, anonymous. I meet

No one I know, but everyone knows me.
My black hat and my black vest, the free

Swing of my guns, the dust that my boots raise,
Here at high noon on this wide road, appraise

All values now, this black against that light.
The glinting gray of steel, black powder, white

When it has turned to smoke, examine you,
When thought has turned to act, when to the true

Exact commission you have put your hand
And muscle follows the exact command.

Remember me. I am the final test
Of everything you know and care for. Jest

And the large gesture count for nothing here.
You are alone, and you have only fear

And hardihood to tell you how to choose.
And you will draw on me, and you will lose.

Letters Home

Old friends, guerillas in their middle age,
Send bombs to all the world in a late rage
Of sinister abandon, and become,
Too soon, too morbidly themselves. Yet some
Give in to madness, alcohol, and death,
And others try indifference, the cold breath
Of the hard drugs, pain, and monastic Zen.
There is no living in some otherwhen,
And these are what we have, eaters of doom,
Carriers of real disaster. Lenses zoom,
And they're immortalized on the late news,
As dead and useless as Masada's Jews,
Fixed in their rage and anger; or alive
And perilous, sectarians of strife,
The prophets of a terror once unknown.
These horrors of the household are our own,
Our sons and brothers, we the Frankenstein
Who bred this flesh for fire and for pine.

In the Marina

The yachts slip down the channel out to sea,
The sky all empty blue, the water white
Where the sun glints or restive wind breaks free,
Lofting the fiery spume into the light.

I stand on shore, where my binoculars
Enlarge minute, lay figures on the decks,
And I can see them hoist the lines and spars
To set all sails, as their bronze muscles flex.

A young man working there seems all alone
In concentration on his purposes
As he moves forward to the shroud lines' groan
And the slow heave of water past his bows.

He is not sailing to the world's far ends.
He gives hard strength and passion in mere play,
And Avalon is all that he intends
This hot, bright afternoon. But on his way,

He travels over depths he cannot gauge
With charts now innocent of reef and shoal
In his companionship with wind and wave
That seem as friendly as his evening goal.

He is not yet upon high seas, where storm
May rend his sheets and scatter his firm mast,
And shatter, too, the powerful young form
That moves so lightly, now the shrouds are fast.

The Chart House

I leave the warm bar and the friendly warmth
Of conversation with young men and old
Whose names I know, whose teachers I have known,
And whose ambitious futures or whose pasts
I have approved in talking with them nightly.
Hunched down and chill, I cross the empty streets,
Hurrying toward the parking lot. And there,
Walking the other way, a tall young man,
His face lit up by chance, smiles openly,
And not in friendship, since I know it is
The thing itself, availability.
And I walk by, giving him no response,
Shaken by choices I can't understand.

You will walk on through the cold streets; and I
Will drive in my own car to my own house
And light the fire, and think about your life,
Bound to casual sex with casual strangers.
And what is there to say of you who search
Waste places after dark? You might have been
My brother or my son, but you are neither.
No one can say what you will ever be,
Young man or old, who navigate the night,
Your eyes not on the street signs nor the stars,
Your destination change. The maps you read
In your smooth mind are atlases of chance.

A Roof in Islamabad

Soldier, what do you see from your high porch?
The great Himalayas, shining in the east,
The Jhelum, roaring like a furious torch
And far below you as it sluices west

To join the Indus on the valley plain?
Or are you watching the long milling sheds,
Where generations labored to sustain
A life too meagre for your innocence

To grasp from such a height? You could not see
The wrath of empire pouring down the hills
Out of the Khyber Pass. Your history
Is not so long nor deep. You have your skills,

As they who filled the pass for centuries
With infantry and archers, sword and gun,
With greave and saber and artillery.
The skills of uniform and discipline

Are real and they are yours. You could not see
The wrath of rumor, till the violent mob
Swarmed in the compound down below, nor see
The bullet with your death. You did your job,

You stood as they had stood, soldiers before,
Who filed down the long pass onto the plain
And formed in their strict ranks, angry and sore
And stood and suffered there the swift, last pain.

Moscow Suburban Nights

I loved you. Now what more is there to say?
Numbed with sleep and the need of sleep, I keep
No dreams nor memories of dreams. I knew
What I had done—in anger in the dark
Smashed the alarm clock on the bedroom floor,
Shouted you down until you broke in terror,
Trembling with pain and fear in the cold night
And inconsolable. Who could forgive,
Or trust, the violent ineptitude,
The clumsy passion of a clown in love?
What did I want that I could not have had
From others at less cost to you and me?
What did you fail to give me, even then,
When anything at all is an abundance,
A frugal bounty to the undeserving?
That government is best which kills the least,
That love is best which governs not at all.

But now the anguish of lost time descends
As physical as pain or the crude power
Of your caress, revisits me like shame,
Or modesty, confusing and confused,
Like the least understood of all our hates,
Unwanted and unneeded and intense.
Lost opportunity, like an abandoned notebook—
All pages blank after the one last page,
No purpose forward and no meaning now—
Defines us wholly in our solitude,
And mind becomes the prison it denies,
As free as air and bound to the ignorance
Of a dead past, errors, unchangeable
And unforgivable. Take the dead leaves,
File them again in their imperfect book,
And let the dust resettle on its edges.

Los Angeles Place Names

I. THE GOOD LIFE

MARINA DEL REY
They are a puzzle. One could say of them,
"So beautiful, merely for being young,"
But they are youth with joy and energy,
Athletically enjoying their new music,
As earlier the surf, and volleyball,
The sun and sand. And they possess this place
As they possess themselves; their movements say,
"We like ourselves, and the serenity
Of sensuous surrender, like our place,
Our time, and we will use them very well."
They are another race, another mind,
Sprung into being here. They are beyond
The charm of the unformed, the yet to be,
Upon whose surfaces our needs impose
A definition of our longing.
                         Youth,
Possessed of the assurance of its need,
Secure in liberty, must look like this.
And watching them, I think that they must feel
No doubt, no fear, no guilt, but tenderness,
Affection, warmth.
                  But who am I to say,
I who am alien to their young lives?
Theirs is not any present I can use,

Because it is my past; and they are locked
Within a future I can never reach.
What would I say to them or they to me?
I have no wisdom that they need as yet.
Though I am out of place by twenty years,
There is some pleasure in my sitting here,
Watching the young and beautiful at play.
Golden children, all the long afternoon,
Till diamond chips sift down the evening sky.

BEL AIR HOTEL

The beautiful may be encountered here,
But they may not be used. This is all *luxe,*
Not *volupté.* The rich take care of that
In other ways. This is for talk with friends,
And not a place to make them or make out.
The drinks are large, the room is warm and quiet,
The lights are low, the service dignified,
But not obsequious and never fast.
This is luxury, and this chair, its lap.
Nothing absurd will ever happen here,
Not even death would dare walk through these doors.

GATSBY'S (WEST LOS ANGELES)

This is the great Good Life! Money and youth,
And places where they both can be enjoyed,
And public admiration for them, too.
Who's giving it away? America
To her fake aristocracy, Show Biz,

Who take the gift with passion and aplomb.
Some greater enterprise might well have claimed
Their ardor and their energy; but think,
And then thank God, they put no pen to paper,
Nor paint to brush, these plumbers of the arts.
Yet who are we to be so fierce with them
Except for envy or for jealousy—
To have contempt for talent, though it's small?
They do no harm, not even to themselves.
They use their virtues well, their youth, their looks,
And their extensive charm, their great good will.
If what they give is not quite art nor science—
No object of enduring contemplation—
Still it would seem an innocent diversion
In a world that's been at war for forty years.
Who can be condescending in a graveyard?
These were the splendors of the Floating World,
Actors and courtesans and rich young men,
The privileged by power or by fame.
We have them, too; and though one might have been
The Tokugawa who created them,
The Utamuro who recorded them,
Someone must be the subject for them both.

WEST HOLLYWOOD
Here, we are told, we find the city's best,
A bottomless, topless, go-go discotheque.
Where barmaids in their scandalous, baroque
Articulations of their surfaces
Move with a mannequin's austerity,

Remote and chill. Music is mindless here,
With the insistent mindlessness of sex,
As they grind out the motions of the brothel
With all a whore's indifference to her trade.
The neighborhood adonises cavort
Between the dart board and the pool room
With Roman noses, with their grecian asses
Stuffed into jeans like sailors in tight whites.

Sit here a while, or sit here long enough.
And it will seem both commonplace
And usual, since every bar constructs
Its special ambiance of approbation.
Values and standards shift; but in this bar,
For this one tribe, this is the absolute,
These are their norms. You are not wanted here.

IN A QUEER COUNTRY (HOLLYWOOD)
Another culture and another shock!
No passports issued, no elections held,
This is a country of the odd extreme,
Where border guards are loose and pass you in,
But rarely pass you back. Who comes here comes,
Less as a tourist than a resident,
Always on sufferance, never quite at home.
The denizens are either rich or poor;
Louche and farouche, the young; the old,
Roué and grey. If no democracy,
It is not quite anarchic brotherhood.
The politics of faction govern here

Where mods and rockers, toughs and puffs contend
For converts to their beaches and their beds.
They are the visible inhabitants,
Violent, colorful, the picaresque
Their mode and principle. Though obvious,
And though the country takes its name from them,
They're not the common man, whose uniform
Is a complex invisibility,
Whose disappearance if you look too close
Perhaps explains his choice and his success
In quiet, if the not quite dull, professions:
Teacher, professor, spy, librarian,
Teller and waiter, poet, painter, pimp.

    SATYR (CHUCK'S, WESTWOOD)
"My horny feet are cutting through the fog,
Which is no fog to me; my medium,
My element is their ambiguous
Relation to the other. Who are they?
I know and you know they are those who need
Just what I have to give them at this moment.
I concentrate the fog to clarity,
I hold them to the motions of one will.
If afterwards, they drift in fog again,
Or if they don't remember, who could care,
Who has regrets, knowing the joys that rise
The more intense for being unregarded.
Listen, my hooves are sharp upon the stones,
Their sounds are questions, opportune, intent.
Assuage your curiosity! You need
Their answers in the fundamental act."

II. DOWN AT THE LOCAL

THE LOCAL
You sit and have a beer. The mostly pleasant,
Congenial hurly-burly of mixed types—
For whom this is a larger living room,
More varied or less lonely than their own—
Excludes by some obscure sodality
The casual, the misfit, and the bore.
Potato chips and pretzels and some beer!
What boozy camaraderie it is,
Or seems to be, until you look again,
Until you see. It is the maimed who come here,
Widowed, divorced, or unattached, the lost,
The lonely, the deserted. Time at the local
Is less a pleasure than a way of life,
Since this is where they live, where they belong,
Where they are known and welcomed every night.
Their needs have been refined to this, this bar,
This night, this recognition of their name.

A STRANGER IN THE LOCAL
This is not quite the bar you should be in.
Over your drink, by your tense attitude
You ask me if I like you, if our lives
Are not alike, if you are not a friend.
Yet, if you are, you are in such a way
As interests no one that I care to know
And least of all myself. I know the men
Who'd find you interesting, who for a time

Would find diversion in your insolence
Of hip and thigh, the thrust and counterthrust
Of mutual availabilities,
Sometimes, perhaps, affection, even trust.
There is the trap for him who would pursue,
The thought that more than surface might be there,
Coupled with such illusion, such allure.
Your question needs an answer: I can say,
No, not a friend, just someone that I met
While sitting in a bar, someone I met.

THE INTELLECTUAL DRUNK
MEDITATES WITH A GLASS OF BEER

He asks, "What is it to hallucinate?"
He answers softly, only to himself,
"To be in a dream, to be deceived, to err,
To take the matter wrong. If sight is lost,
We're blind; if sight receives its objects wrong,
Then we hallucinate; if wilfully,
We choose hallucination to clear sight,
The metamorphoses of alcohol,
Sanctions of feeling from a chemical.
These thresholds are soon old. A common drunk
Knows them as well as I do, so I am
A drunk, searching for new anatomies;
Or once I was. I say that I want love,
But what I love is liquor, sitting here,
And contemplating nothing that I know.
When I drink, the surfaces of the world
Are nothing but the surface that I see;

No depths, no shades, and no complexities
To qualify my seeing. The bar becomes,
Not quite the world that I had most desired,
But one that I can live in comfortably.
And so we sit, amateurs of nirvana,
Slow suicides, afraid of life and death."

    ANOTHER LOCAL (THE CHARTHOUSE)
Westwood, or Coronado, Malibu,
It scarcely matters. They are all the same,
The same appeal to casual luxury,
The same polite and handsome, youthful crew,
Spectacular in their vitality,
Around the margins of whose consciousness
One finds a place to be. They live their lives;
And you have yours, thornier, older, gnarled,
As theirs will someday be. Meanwhile they work,
And you are part of it: they wait on you.
They chat and argue, sometimes they discuss
The bar and business, sports, the books they read,
Life at the beach, their friends, their larger aims.
Acute and commonsensical, they know
More of the world than I did at their age.
They are engaging and respectful. My grey hairs
And my bald head are not ridiculous,
Even to me, in such an atmosphere,
At once intelligent and tolerant.
And one expands a little from the chill
Of more abrasive climates. I relax.
They are so very much themselves that I

Almost become myself, almost let go.
There is a model here. After a time,
We do not change. We learn to bear ourselves,
And bear the burden of our friends, and they,
They bear us too, with equal fortitude.
Our problems are not solved. They are survived
With grace and caution, day by careful day.

Metaphysics at Twenty-Six

The hard edge of the stars
assails him like the thin
edge of the cold, persists
in him like self-pity,
poverty or despair.
He has not surrendered,
but he cannot resist
the charm of self-concern
in the terror of his
disappearance in time.
The theology of
one's dilemma is cold,
luminous, and like that
of the absurd, defines
nothing. It is at last
its own reason, being,
as nothing else is, clear,
empty and absolute—
as it absorbs the mind,
one's energy of action
and all alternatives.

Imperfect Correspondences

1. AT THE BEACH
If I care more than you, then I must pay,
And willingly. On the beach this bright day
Your laughter moves me more than tender speech.
I am in love with you. Your two arms reach
Into a brief extension of the sea.
You play with water as you play with me,
All surface and good nature. So, who cares?
Who cares will pay exactly what he dares.

2. AT A RECITAL
You find it beautiful, I find it dull.
Expectations of more than music differ,
Of sentiment, of love. And so they shall.
And so we are defined. Art should be stiffer
Than real tears. By art we might condense
The waste expansions to the more intense.
This lingers in its ecstasies too long,
It's more a self-indulgence than a song.

3. THIRD LETTER
You speculate in your way, I in mine.
So, if I take you as I take my wine,
It is not you I seek nor mere release
Of passion into numbness. When I cease
To want what you are not, I'll not want you.
For you and I and life will all be through.

4. FOURTH LETTER

We come together in what need and haste,
Need of each other or of someone merely,
Haste to be done, have done, once more? Clearly,
This will not, cannot do. The private, chaste
Interstices of feeling are invaded
With skill and violence. In what recess
Of spirit may I hide and not confess
My utter self until I am degraded?

5. FIFTH LETTER

I know your body. Knowing reaffirms
Selfness, identity, disgust. If Act,
Intended union, mutual reply,
Is unaccompanied, then in whose arms,
In whose strength do you lie? Mere pride would ask
Where have you been, where are you now, when I
Shudder and rest, and you ask, "Are you through?"

6. SIXTH LETTER

I say what I think but you never do
Till injury accumulates to wrath
And wrath becomes the passion that you suffer.
Then is it my fault that I never made
The silences in which you might have spoken,
The places for your reticence? It is,
And is the waste, the loss that I now suffer.

7. SEVENTH LETTER

Nothing was promised! What delirium
Of sense persuaded me that, giving so,
You cared, would give yourself, might love. A fool,
I was a pure occasion for the raw
Feel of experience; your appetite,
Your curiosity require the new
For your sensations. Sleep with all the damned,
Stranger in love. You have embarked on seas
Charted before by crude adventurers
Who took their watery knowledge to the grave.

8. EIGHTH LETTER

A late, a quiet dinner, then the tab
And coffee. I could walk or take a cab
Or have another bourbon in the bar,
The dim locale where columnist and star
And lesser absentees from the workaday
Glitter until closing. Yet if I stay,
If it is late, and I am lonely, free,
What do these strangers have to do with me?
Few are old; most are shrewd; most, beautiful,
Or if not, young, and most available
Tonight, or if not, then tomorrow, say,
In any bar or bed and any way.
Boredom might be the index of a mind,
But they are avid. We find out our kind.
I feel my age. My interest in this place
Is absolute. I turn away my face.

9. WAKING

Your absence summons me from sleep. The light
And silence are companions through the night.
I lie awake, imagining your face
And that you bend to kiss mine, that the place
Beside me that was yours once still is yours
And not an emptiness my heart ignores.
Through pages of a book, grown dim and blurred,
I listen for your step. This is absurd—
Though memory distorts your face and hands,
I moved and still move answering your commands.
Imperfect action and imperfect art
Know their own cause in the imperfect heart.

10. FINALE

All that is past or passing. Now who cares
That I cared? No one but myself. I thought
I wanted what you wanted for yourself;
Food, quiet, rest, affection, your own bed;
To come and go, to stay or not to stay,
Just as it pleased you. Selflessness is proved,
Not by intent, but advent. Absence and loss
Are gifts I would refuse. And all reproach
Is vanity, I know. All angry words,
Pleas, abject tones, and motions of brute pride
Sink to irrelevance. I took my chance
And you took yours, and they were not the same.

Adagia

Stolid and literal, I take my stand.
Art is decision, not the chance, unplanned
Performance of a trivial, vulgar act.
It is selection of the crucial fact.
Though brute particulars still litter sense,
Art's the suppression of irrelevance.
Life is the constant pressure of the new,
But art, the final judgment of the true,
Measures resistance to inane distraction.
Art is the model of coherent action.
It is not my confusion or confession,
It tells you nothing of my worst obsession,
It's not a gossip's tale concerning me:
It is the meaning of my history.
It is constructed and can be construed
As proposition and as attitude.
Then art is structure: nothing can be said
Without the order in which it is read.
Art is technique, by which the masters say
That ends are realized in a métier.
Art is distinction: process is not being.
The words you see are all there is worth seeing.

Measures

A clock cannot say why.
Only the terse and dry
Renewal of its chime,
Beguiling as a rime
In tongues we do not speak,
Tells us the fact we seek.
The clock hangs on the wall
And knows nothing at all,
Nothing at all to say,
Except, "This hour, this day,
This minute that I chime—
There is no other time."
But we know better, we,
In our extremity,
Know we outlive, outpace,
The single moment's race
Toward its extinguishment.
We know our own intent
And with preemptive line,
With words that name, define,
And classify our fear,
We write what you will hear.
Our names are on the words
As flight is in a bird
And form blown into glass.
Our force, our breath, will pass
And fear will die away.
Our words, perhaps, will stay.

Terra Cognita

Who shares my house with me?
The fly, the ant, the bee,

The field mouse and the bird,
Whose fur and down are stirred

By the same wind and rain,
Lashing my window pane.

Who shares the open sky?
White cloud, and blue so high

It treads the mountain ledge
And tilts the granite ridge.

What speaks to me, as near
As old, familiar fear?

The silence of lost friends,
Consumed in angry ends,

Madness, or something more,
Malice, misfortune, war—

Names that involve the air
In motions of despair

Upon the vaulted skies.
What closes up our eyes?

What falls upon our ears?
The dust of all the years,

The earthen floor I tread,
In which I make my bed.

Remembered Landscape

The empty season burns
With frost, and pallid snow
Mounds up the garden urns
To stony crystal. No,

Nothing to see for miles
But waste and wilderness.
Bare trees and blackened piles
Define the white duress

Of ice and icy glare,
The chill of entropy,
The malice of the air
Invading all we see.

This is beyond despair,
Beyond the stoic will
In numbing loss and care—
Nothing is left to kill.

The House of Exile

Death is no riddle, not a mere unknown;
It is unknowable—like Nothing, None.
It is pure absence, no place, nowhere, not,
Negative absolute, the unlived-through.
It is pure evil, the unspecified,
Unspecifiable in any way
By figure, trope or crude analogy.
Using the oldest magic that we know,
We give death vesture, habit, and a name.
We give it entrance with a golden bough
Or stony lintel and a keep of thorns.
We give it locus and mythography
With skies as blue and banal as our own,
And people its dim land with dimmer shades
Forever silent on their distant shore;
Or call it some abstraction of the mind,
Repose, or contemplation, or the good.
In truth, it is imploded space, a name
Which has no definition and no face.